MW00950721

DEDICATED...

To the One from whom all dreams come.

To the two that taught me to dream
(Dad and Mom).

To my little one whose dreams are all fulfilled,

and

To my son Cayden, watching his dreams
take shape and grow.

And a special thank you, to Elizabeth Love.

Your help, and belief in me, made it happen.

THE DAY I LEARNED TO FLY
by Jeffery D. Kennon

ILLUSTRATIONS:
Kristen Lawton ~ Illustrator
Christin King ~ Initial artwork
Merry Dare Goodwin ~ Conceptual artist

The day I learned to fly...

You might not believe this... but the day I learned to fly... wasn't the day I turned 16, 18, 22 or 25...

Believe it or not, I was 8 years old when I really learned to fly.

Growing up, I had two energetic brothers, a mother with spunky red hair, a loving father who wasn't afraid of anything, and a long-eared hound dog named Dixie.

We had the best back yard in the world, with climbing trees and a hill. There was a metal shed my father and "his boys" built. When we slid open those rusty shed doors, a world without limits beckoned us.

It was the metal shed of magic and imagination!

Disappointed lawn mowers, lonely bicycle parts, inner tubes, tools, plastic scraps, screws, left behind pieces of projects from years gone by, and best of all… the items you can build just about anything with, except maybe a submarine…

2x4's, nails and a hammer!

As I said, you can build anything, except maybe a submarine, out of 2x4's, nails and a hammer… trust me.

I don't know about you, but I always dreamed of flying. During class I would imagine I was soaring beyond the limits of what my dad called "Gravity"… the thing that holds us down to the ground. I would stare at the sky and dream of what it must be like to drift along the air currents like a bird.

With the cape of night wrapped around our home, in my mind I would move above the ground, sometimes slow and gentle like a leaf falling from a tree, and other times fast, like a bullet. All it took was for me to stretch my arms out to my sides, close my eyes, and away I would go.

Sometimes I'd wing through the starlight to far away towns, through floating clouds, to visit little cobblestone street villages ~ but usually I would orbit the sky above our town. I didn't like going far from my mother, father and brothers.

When not dreaming about flying, my brothers and I always longed for a go kart… with an engine, a real steering wheel, brakes, and seat belts. But our mother was convinced someone would get seriously hurt, so we had to build one ourselves.

We started our go kart venture by designing a push kart.

A push kart is a go kart WITHOUT an engine.

We constructed our speedy craft in the metal shed of magic and imagination.

We used an old piece of plywood for the floor, supported by 2x4's. You can build almost anything, except maybe a submarine, out of 2x4's, nails and a hammer… trust me.

With these pieces in place, the body of our push kart came alive; strong, sturdy and ready for speed.

To tell you about the axles I will have to give away our trade secret. The boy-built axles were a wonder to behold. Yes, you guessed it, we took another 2x4 that was 3 ½ feet long. We nailed this at the rear so it was sideways across the body of the push kart, and now for the secret...

We used discarded lawn mower wheels that lived in the shed of magic and imagination.

4 plastic wheels volunteered; 2 large, and 2 small.

It would have been best to have a steel rod to mount them on, but none lurked in our shed of magic and imagination.

Our piggy bank, which we filled by doing chores around the house, fell short of the cost.

So… the secret…

We hammered 4 nails bunched together, through the center hole of each wheel into the 2x4 so the wheels could spin on our homemade, trade secret, nail axle.

Before we knew it… we had large back wheels mounted.

The front axle was a little more complicated… You see, the front axle has to let you steer, and this means it has to pivot so the kart will turn on command just like a car.

After careful consideration, and rummaging through all of the left behind parts in the shed of magic and imagination, we found a large bolt, washers and a nut. This would allow us to mount the front axle on the body of the kart so it would pivot for turning.

Yes, you guessed it. We started with another 2x4 laid flat under the front end of the kart. We drilled a hole in the center of both the 2x4 and the plywood floor of the push kart body. Then we mounted the 2x4 so that it could pivot around the bolt which was held into place by the nut and washers.

We mounted the front wheels just like the rear wheels.

The wheels came alive, as if they wanted to roll, wanted to move… they wanted to take us places we'd only dreamed of in our imagination.

I thought it would leap off the ground like a horse in a race. It was sleek, fast, and dangerous looking. I could almost see steam, like hot breath, coming from the front of the push kart as if it was saying, "Lets roll!"

The next question was, "How are we going to steer it?"

Then I remembered in the old Westerns we used to watch, all horses were steered by something called "reins".

We decided to use the same thing.

A few feet of rope tied to each end of the front axle would allow the driver to guide the kart where he wanted it to go.

We could pull on the right side of the rope and the kart would turn right. The same would happen with the left side of the rope for the left turn.

The last few items were:

a seat

brakes

and a special emergency brake.

The seat was easy… just a piece of wood propped up with… yes, you guessed it, a small 2x4 nailed to the body and the back of the seat.

The only issue was that the nails would stick through the seat and poke you in the back, but it worked.

For some reason, I don't know why… brakes were really important to us. We decided on two methods for stopping our vehicle: a main brake, and an emergency brake.

The main brake was a 2x4 cut to about 12 inches long, and nailed in the middle, to the side of the push kart body.

When you pulled up on one end of the 2x4, the other end would scrape against the ground, stopping the kart.

You can build almost anything, except maybe a submarine, out of 2x4's, nails and a hammer… trust me.

For the emergency brake, which I believe was inspired by my favorite cartoons, we tied a cinder block to the push kart, carried it on the rear, and in case of an emergency, threw it off as dead weight.

Surely, the dragging cinder block plus the hand brake would counter the massive speeds I would reach!

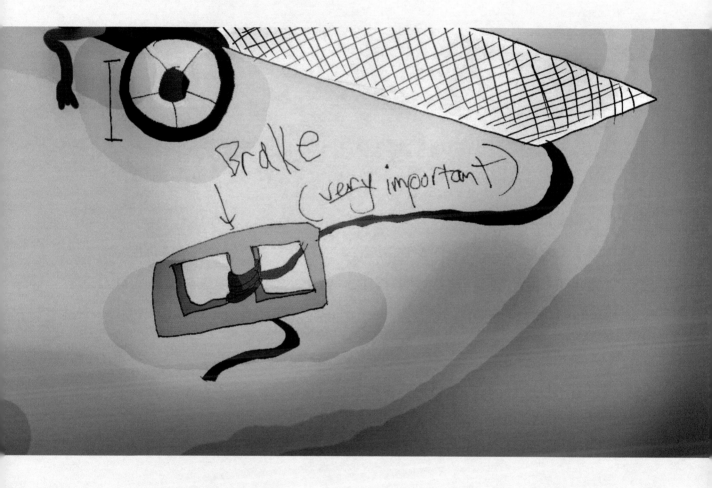

The next day, I was sitting in the push kart, ready to take her on our first trial run, when…

I gazed into the blue sky as an airplane streaked overhead, and started dreaming of what it must be like to actually fly.

As I sat there, I imagined my push kart having wings… powerful, strong supportive wings… wings that could lift me up through any weather, and to any heights.

My runway was the street we lived on. Our first flight could be around our own neighborhood!

I saw myself coasting down our street, picking up speed while holding the steering reins in my hands. I could feel the strength of my push kart, ready to climb like a homesick angel to the clouds above.

As I came off the ground I kept a straight course 'till I gained enough height, and then banked over my house while leaning into the turn.

What a feeling to be free, and to be above the ground!

Without warning my mother called, "What are you doing?"

I guess, seeing me, unmoving, sitting in the driver's seat, staring at the sky, doing 'nothing', caught her attention.

"Oh, just playing...," which was my standard line for everything, but this brought me back down to earth.

So, now that I was sitting in the cockpit of my go kart - turned airplane… how could I make it fly?

In order to fly, our kart would need wings.

I had flown in my imagination dozens of times, looking out over the front yard, from my second story window. Everything felt magical from there.

While thinking about that, I remembered that we had window screens. They were about 4 feet long by 2 ½ feet wide and…

would be perfect for wings!

I leapt up, ran into the house, and headed upstairs.

As I breezed through the kitchen my mother called, "Jeff, what are you doing?"

"Just playing," I said as I kept moving - up to their bedroom where I unhooked the window screen from its nail, and let it float to the ground.

I was shocked! IT WAS TRUE… screens made perfect wings because it floated down, picked up speed, and landed flat all by itself!

It… was… a… wing!

23

So off to my bedroom where I did the same thing there. Within 5 minutes I had the wings (screens), by the push kart ready for mounting.

Now, I am no dummy. I knew that I needed to cover these wings with something that would seal them from letting air move through them, since that is what screens were designed for.

So off I went once more to the shed of magic and imagination. There in a pile, like a used jacket, were sheets of thin plastic. I drafted them to our service, cut them to length, wrapped the screens, and taped them down. (Surely, tape would hold.)

After both wings were completed, it was time to mount them.

Falling back to my old standard of 2x4's, nails and a hammer, which you can build practically anything out of, except maybe a submarine - I cut 2 small pieces about 4 inches long, and mounted them under where my knees would be.

With the wings now mounted, my vision began taking flight.

The image in my mind was living, breathing, straining for the sky and clouds.

How could I keep her down?

I called her, "her", because I had seen my dad pat his old car one day when it wouldn't start and say, "Sweetheart, be a good girl for me, and start up,"… and it started!

So my aircraft must be a girl too!

I knew it would fly… I knew it would work.

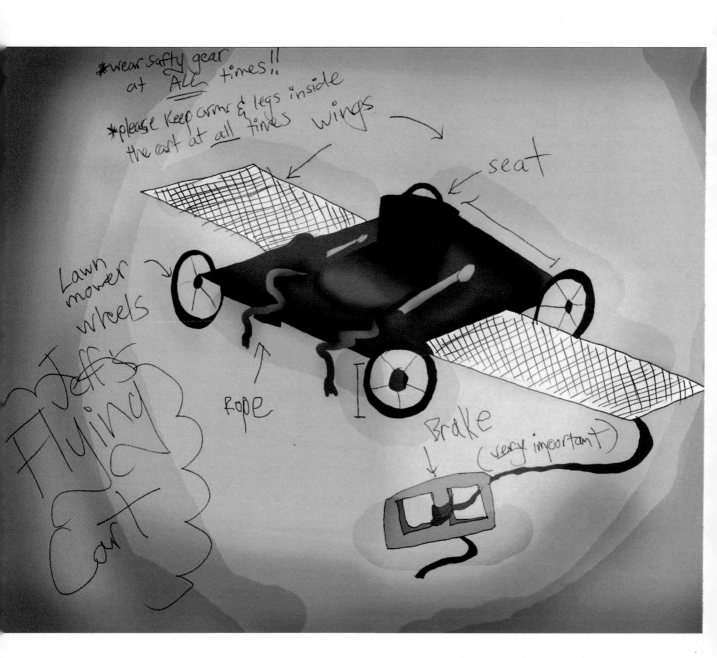

*wear safty gear
at ALL times!!

*please keep arms & legs inside
the cart at all times   wings

seat

Lawn
mower
wheels

Jeff's
Flying
Cart

rope

Brake   (very important)

I was going to need protective gear for my first flight.

One of my favorite things to play with was my father's old football helmet. It was actually leather, and had a hole on each side for the ears. No one ever knew it was a football helmet, and I had told friends it was a fighter pilot's helmet from the OLD days.

I ran inside, got my pilot's helmet, and then went downstairs to the junk room and picked up my mom's white garden gloves which had strawberries on them. These were the only gloves available to protect me at high altitudes, so strawberries it was.

I then called my friend Alan and informed him I was about to take to the sky, and could use his help in becoming famous. Then I ran, like a rabbit, back out the door.

I walked to my trusty steed, my winged machine of speed, heard the breeze flap its way against the plastic covered wings and just knew…

I… was… about… to… fly…

I patted her and said, "That's a good girl."

Alan rode up, greeted me, and after one look, proclaimed "she" would fly, and we ~ he and I, would be famous. He inspected my work and found nothing amiss at all.

I said, "Let's take her up to the top of the street, let her roll down, pick up speed, and by my calculations, (which were done by guessing) I should be airborne by the time I reach my driveway."

He agreed and off we went.

We did however, run into a little snag…

Now that my bird of prey had her wings extended, we couldn't get the aircraft though our back yard gate. However, boy power prevailed, and with grit we lifted her up and over the fence.

I knew…

I… was… about… to… fly…

There were a few neighbors who looked at us as we walked our marvelous machine up the hill. The road had a slight bend that would block our view of the house from the top, but I wasn't worried. Alan would make sure the coast was clear for me 'till I came into view.

My other thought was that if any obstructions got by… well, I would just lean back, and off we would fly a little early. Zooming over obstacles sounded fun anyway, so I wasn't concerned.

Once situated at the top of the hill, Alan assisted me as I put on my helmet, and mom's garden gloves. (Somehow strawberries didn't seem to fit a pilot, but whatever...)

Then I seated myself and tied a rope around my waist, so the g-force wouldn't throw me out.

Alan ran down the hill with instructions to holler when he was ready, and the runway was clear.

Here I was. I couldn't believe it…

In just a matter of seconds, I would be flying above the cars, houses, my yard, Dixie the hound dog, our tree house, and then…

… the neighborhood kids would come out by the dozens, scream and shout at me, their mothers would gasp in shock and the fathers would nudge each other and say things like, "Jeff's something else, ain't he!"

My heart was racing, sweat poured down my face and into the moist leather helmet. Mom's strawberry garden gloves were damp from the tension. I was about to join the elite, the few, the brave list of 8 year olds who flew!

I waited as the sweat stung my eyes. The sun was behind me, and the way was clear for an early afternoon take off.

It was then I heard it, "Yahooooo" from Alan...

It was time...

I put my feet down, and started to do what the un-trained, non-pilot types, might call 'awkward leg movements', to get the kart moving. But those really 'in the know' would see the strides like a mighty Pegasus preparing for the sky.

Slowly my winged beast started to move. I lifted my feet and placed them on the front axle, and held onto the rope preparing for the blast of speed and light as I shot into the air!

The plastic lawn mower wheels rumbled and growled as they wobbled on their super secret, should be patented, nails-for-an-axle. Ever so slightly, the plastic began to ripple on the wings and I knew...

I... was... about... to... fly...

I had to be up to a blistering 4 miles per hour, when I rounded the corner and saw Alan, ten driveways down from me, waving his hands.

Parked cars were starting to flash by faster and faster. The plastic was rippling with the power of the wind. The perspiration was no longer dripping down my face, but starting to stream back into the leather helmet and I knew…

I… was… about… to… fly…

My speed continued to climb, and I noticed the tape that held the wing covering on, was starting to fray and come apart. I didn't falter, quaver, or change my plans.

It was do, die, or fly, and fly was the only option.

Eight driveways to go, and the wings were starting to move…

Time seemed to slow down, as if I was pushing through the time barrier itself in my winged eagle.

Five driveways and my flight would begin. I could feel the rush of air, the sound of birds joining me, the mist of clouds against my face… it was going to happen.

The speed was picking up, and the wings were beginning to strain against the nails as she reached for the sky. I could feel the plastic tires get lighter on the pavement and their wobbling noise was getting less as speed and lift increased.

I was two driveways away when my wings started to strain against the air pressure. Some unseen force was trying to keep me earth bound.

We were breaking every speed record ever set by 8 year old pilots.

Lawn mower wheels across the world dreamed of going this fast.

No piece of rope ever flapped in the breeze as fast as my steering rope shook!

Just as I passed Alan it happened… faster than I could have imagined…

There was a loud vibrating crack, and both wings went straight up, folded and bent where they hit each other like the clapping of hands over and around my head. I couldn't see because the wings (screens), folded over me like someone wrapping my head in a blanket.

I reached for the main brake, threw out the emergency cinder block, and heard it bumping and scraping down the pavement behind me, as I prayed for a quick stop.

My eyes were still covered, but as far as I could tell, the only thing that stopped me, was the curb.

With another crack and crash the kart and I ended up in the neighbor's front yard, dragging a smaller cinder block than when I started, wings wrapped around my head, and the front axle now underneath the seat.

All was still… quiet… and then the realization hit me.

I didn't fly…

I was not looking down over the top of the house.

Kids were not running underneath me screaming. Dads were not talking about me, and there were no clouds, no birds… just grass, and plastic wafting slowly in the breeze.

Alan came running and helped me untangle myself. I looked at him, and he looked at me with shock and sadness.

We carried, pushed, pulled, and begged the old push kart back over the fence to the shed of magic and imagination, in the back yard.

We placed the front wheels under the kart. Alan said he needed to go, and without another word, got on his bike and pedaled out.

I was beginning to wonder how I would explain the bent window screens, the marks on the pavement from the cinder block, to my mom and dad, and any possible adult who saw me try to kill myself!

I felt like such a failure, as I sat down on the old kart... when it hit me...

... like a slow dawning of realization, or a curtain being pulled open...

I closed my eyes, and saw myself with the clouds, the birds, the small figures of kids running underneath me, the tops of the houses; feeling the bank of my craft as we turned into the wind... and then I understood...

Using my imagination... dreaming... was true flight.

Many years later I became a pilot.

But this was the day I learned to fly… beyond the reaches of where the go kart wings could have ever carried me.

Made in the USA
Charleston, SC
06 February 2016